In a wood next to a big river, there lived a fox and a stork. One morning, they met on the bank of the river. "Come and have some dinner with me," said the fox to the stork. "Yes, thank you, I will," replied the stork.

So the fox set about cooking dinner.
He mixed, cut, chopped, and added
until he had made a big pot of food.
"Mmmm, that smells good," said the
fox. He looked into the pot
and licked his lips.

When the stork arrived, she said,
“Mmmm, that smells good. I did not
catch much fish this morning,
so I am very hungry.

The fox and the stork sat down to dinner. The fox spooned out the food onto the big, flat plates he had set out.

The stork pecked at the food with her long, pointed bill, but it was hard for her as the plate was so flat. She pecked and pecked, but she only ate a little of her food.

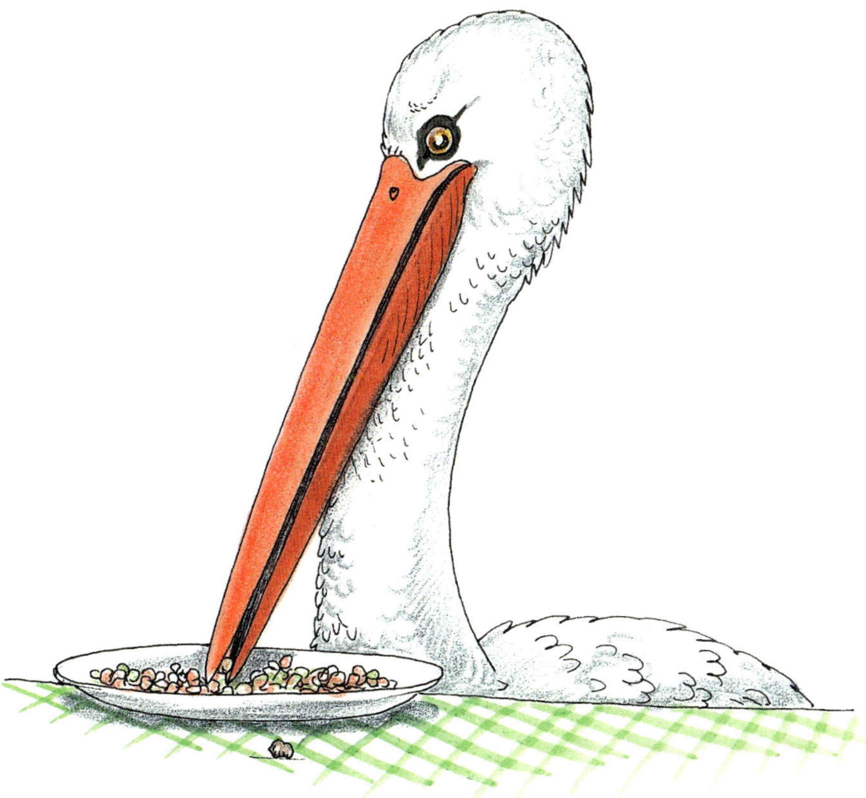

When he had finished his dinner,
the fox licked his lips.
"Mmmm, that was good," he said.
"Have you finished?" he added,
looking at the stork's plate.

"My bill is too long and pointed for this big, flat plate," the stork explained. She was still very hungry, and it made her angry when the fox quickly ate all the food she had left as well.

The next week, when the fox came to the river bank, he found the stork there, waiting for him.

"Will you come and have dinner with me this evening?" she said.
"Yes, thank you, I will," said the fox, licking his lips greedily.
"I am so glad," said the stork politely, but she smiled to herself.

This time, it was the stork who cooked the dinner. She mixed, cut, chopped, and added until she had made a big pot of food.
"Mmmm," the stork said to herself. "That smells good."

When the fox arrived,
he sniffed the food cooking.
"Mmmm," he said, "that smells good.
I am hungry," and he rubbed his belly.

The stork and the fox sat down to dinner. The stork spooned out the food into the tall, thin jars she had set out.

The fox tried to lick his food out of the top of the jar, but it was hard for him as the jar was so tall and thin.
He licked and licked, but he only ate a little of his food.

He had to sit and see the stork peck up all her dinner with her long, thin bill. "Mmmm. That was good," she said. "Have you finished?" she added, looking at all the food the fox had left.

"I cannot lick more. This jar is too tall and thin for me," he explained.

The greedy fox was angry when the stork finished up the rest of the food in his jar. He still felt hungry as he had had so little dinner.

"Well," the stork said, "I was upset when I came to dinner with you, and you gave me a big, flat plate."

"I am sorry," the fox said. "It was wrong of me. Come and have dinner with me again next week, and this time will be different."

So next week, the stork went to have dinner with the fox again. Before she arrived, the fox chopped, cut, added, and mixed, until he had a big pot of food.

"Mmmm, that smells good," he said.

When the stork arrived, she smiled and said, “That smells good.”
“Thank you. Come and sit down,” said the fox.”

He set out a big, flat plate for himself again, but he gave the stork a tall, thin jar. This time she had no problem getting at her food, and she ate plenty!